This

THOMAS & FRIENDS ™

Annual belongs to

_____

SODOR № 1 RAILWAY

ANNUAL 2012

CONTENTS

EGMONT
We bring stories to life

First published in Great Britain 2011 by Egmont UK Limited
239 Kensington High Street, London W8 6SA
All rights reserved.

Written by Pippa Shaw. Designed by Suzanne Cooper.
ISBN 978 1 4052 5707 7
10 9 8 7 6 5 4 3 2 1
Printed in Italy

HiT entertainment

MEET MY FRIENDS

1

THE FAT CONTROLLER

The Fat Controller is the director of the Railway and makes sure everything runs on time. His real name is Sir Topham Hatt.

JAMES

With his splendid red paint and a golden number 5 on his side, James is always easy to spot as he puffs around the Island.

PERCY

Percy is Thomas' best friend! It's his job to deliver the mail, and he is never late.

EMILY

Emily can be a little bossy sometimes, but her heart is always in the right place.

HENRY

Henry is a Really Useful Engine because he is long and fast! He's happy to help anyone in need.

EDWARD

Like Thomas, Edward has beautiful blue paint. He is number 2, and has his own branch line from Brendam to Wellsworth.

GORDON

Fast and strong, Gordon has the special job of pulling the Express. He uses his speed and strength to help others, too.

CHARLIE

Cheeky Charlie is an engine from the mainland who loves to have fun and is always ready for adventure.

BERTIE

Beep beep! Here comes Bertie. He's as Really Useful as any Engine, and loves driving around Sodor's beautiful roads.

TOBY

Toby is the number 7 brown tram engine. He loves to keep busy and usually works at the Quarry.

DIESEL

Diesel loves to stir up trouble in the shed by saying that diesels are better than steamies. But he can be Really Useful, too.

HAROLD

Who's that flying high in the sky? It's Harold! He's a member of the Sodor Search and Rescue Team and always keeps a watchful eye out for his friends.

VICTOR

Victor runs the Sodor Steamworks, where he fixes broken engines, finds spare parts and helps any engines in need. He always has a big smile on his face.

KEVIN

Kevin also works at the Steamworks. He's always happy to lend a helping hook, though sometimes he gets too excited, which can lead to trouble!

ROSIE

Despite her pretty purple paint, Rosie is a real tomboy! She thinks Thomas is the best and likes to copy his every move.

HIRO

Hiro is one of the oldest engines on Sodor. He was once known as the 'Master of the Railway', but Thomas found him abandoned on an old section of track!

CRANKY

Cranky the crane spends his days loading and unloading at Brendam Docks. He can be a bit gruff, but he keeps everything running smoothly.

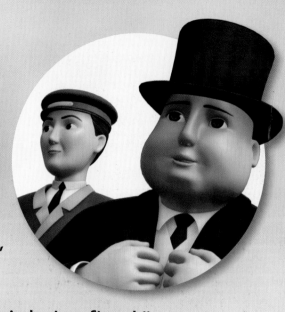

One day, The Fat Controller was looking very serious indeed.

"Percy has popped a piston, Thomas," he told the little blue engine. "You must deliver the mail for him tomorrow while he is being fixed."

"Yes, Sir!" smiled Thomas.

After he had finished his jobs that afternoon, Thomas stopped off to see Percy. He was at the Steamworks, waiting to be repaired.

"Do you want me to tell you what to do with the mail, Thomas?" Percy asked.

"Delivering the mail is easy, Percy," came Thomas' reply. "I know what to do!" And with that he puffed off to Tidmouth Sheds for a good night's sleep. He had to be up very early in the morning!

The next day dawned clear and bright. While all the other engines were still fast asleep, Thomas chuffed cheerfully around the Island. At every stop, he blew his whistle to let the managers know he had arrived. **Peep! Peep!**

At the Quarry, he woke up Mavis from her peaceful sleep. At Brendam Docks, he made such a noise that Cranky woke up! And at the Steamworks, his whistling woke Kevin with a jump. But Thomas was having too much fun to notice that he was waking his friends. He whistled louder with every stop he made!

Soon, all the mail was delivered and Thomas decided to tell Percy what a good job he had done.

As he passed the Quarry, he saw Mavis' trucks being loaded with slate. But Mavis hadn't lined up her trucks properly under the hopper, and the slate spilled all over the floor.

"That's strange," Thomas said to himself. "Mavis never makes mistakes."

What Thomas didn't know was that Mavis was so tired she had fallen asleep with her trucks in the wrong place!

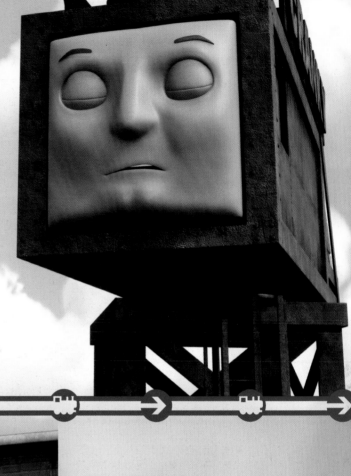

He chuffed on past the Docks. Cranky was lifting heavy barrels from a big ship, but he dropped them all with a crash.

"How odd," Thomas said to himself. "Cranky never makes mistakes." What Thomas hadn't seen was that Cranky was fast asleep after being woken so early.

As Thomas entered the Steamworks, he couldn't see Percy anywhere. But he could see The Fat Controller, looking very cross.

"Percy still isn't fixed because someone woke Kevin up too early this morning by tooting loudly on their whistle. The same someone woke up Mavis and Cranky too. Now, all these engines have made silly mistakes!" The Fat Controller said.

Thomas felt awful. He knew it was his cheerful whistling that had woken everyone up.

"I'm sorry, Sir," he said to The Fat Controller. "I promise I will do a better job tomorrow."

That night, Thomas went to visit Percy again. This time, he listened to everything Percy had to tell him about delivering the mail.

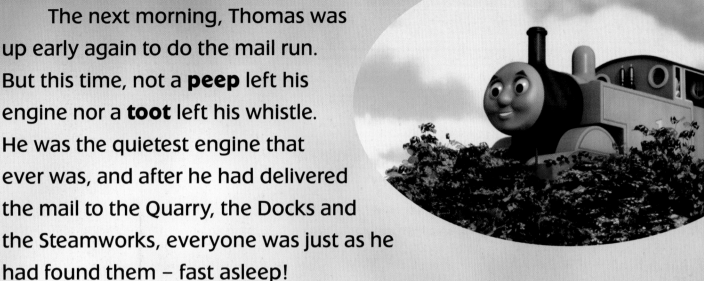

The next morning, Thomas was up early again to do the mail run. But this time, not a **peep** left his engine nor a **toot** left his whistle. He was the quietest engine that ever was, and after he had delivered the mail to the Quarry, the Docks and the Steamworks, everyone was just as he had found them – fast asleep!

Everyone, that is, except Percy. He was so proud of his friend that he had woken up early to say what a good job he had done.

"Thank you, Percy," Thomas smiled as he fell asleep. Delivering the mail was harder than he'd thought, but Thomas had proved he was a Really Useful Engine!

Now that you have read all about Thomas' adventure delivering the mail, see if you can answer these questions about it. Circle the right answers to the questions below.

1 Which engine usually delivers the mail?

a Spencer   **b Percy**   **c Toby**

2 When did Thomas set off?

a Morning   **b Afternoon**   **c Night-time**

3 Who did Thomas wake up at the Steamworks?

a James

b Kevin

c Hiro

4 Where was Percy being repaired?

a Tidmouth Sheds

b Sodor Slate Quarry

c The Steamworks

5 Who dropped the slate at the Quarry?

a Mavis

b Diesel

c James

DOUBLE TROUBLE

One day, Thomas was happily puffing to Maithwaite Station. This was no ordinary day though. It was The Fat Controller's birthday, and Thomas had to take him to his grand party.

As Thomas pulled up to the platform, his brakes shrieked in shock. The Fat Controller had grown a moustache!

"Thomas! My good friend!" The Fat Controller greeted him.

This was very strange indeed. Thomas had never heard The Fat Controller call him his 'good friend' before, and he'd certainly never seen The Fat Controller with a moustache!

"We've got lots of time before the party, Thomas," boomed The Fat Controller. "Let's go to the Whispering Woods."

Now Thomas was even more puzzled. He wanted to ask if something strange had happened, but he didn't want to look silly.

"The Fat Controller must just be very excited about his party," Thomas told himself. Then The Fat Controller climbed on board Annie and they chuffed away to the Whispering Woods.

From then on, The
Fat Controller's behaviour
got stranger. When
they reached the
Whispering Woods,
he ran among the
trees, playing
hide-and-seek with the
children whom Edward
was taking to the party. The
two engines watched him, amazed.

"I've never seen The Fat Controller play hide-and-seek,
Thomas," Edward said.

"I know," Thomas replied. "Today, The Fat Controller doesn't seem like The Fat Controller at all!"

But although his wheels were wobbling with worry, Thomas didn't ask any questions. He was still too scared of looking silly. After the game had finished, The Fat Controller climbed back on board Annie and they clickety-clacked back to Maithwaite. Thomas was relieved because he didn't want The Fat Controller to be late for his own party.

But when they stopped at a red light, The Fat Controller leapt down and climbed into the signalling box! He started pulling levers and pushing buttons, so when Gordon came past carrying party guests, he was sent down the wrong track!

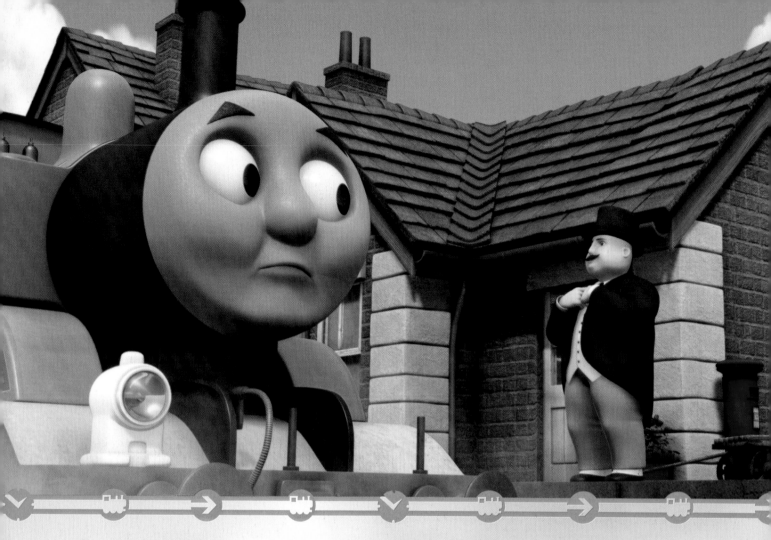

The Fat Controller climbed down from the box, chuckling.

Now Thomas knew something was wrong. When they reached Maithwaite, Thomas found the courage to ask the question that had been bothering him.

"Excuse me, Sir" he said, "but are you The Fat Controller?"

"Goodness, no!" the man laughed. "I'm his brother, Sir Lowham Hatt!"

Just then, the Stationmaster ran towards Thomas.

"Where were you?" he asked. "The Fat Controller and Lady Hatt had to go to the party on Bertie, but they haven't arrived yet. Neither have Edward or Gordon with their passengers."

Thomas was upset. If he had found out about The Fat Controller's brother earlier then none of this would have happened.

"Bertie must have broken down!" he cried. "We must find him quickly."

"Hurrah, more hide-and-seek!" cheered Sir Lowham as they puffed away to find The Real Fat Controller.

Thomas found Bertie by the side of the road, with smoke coming out of his engine. The Fat Controller was standing next to him.

"Thomas, where have you been?" he asked crossly.

Thomas was about to tell him when Sir Lowham appeared and explained, laughing at the mischief he had caused. The Fat Controller didn't find it very funny at all, and still looked very cross as he and Lady Hatt climbed aboard Annie.

Thomas whizzed along the rails and delivered his passengers to the party. But Thomas couldn't stay – he still had work to do!

He chuffed to the Whispering Woods, to tell Edward all about The Fat Controller's brother.

"Go straight to the party with the children, Edward!" Thomas urged him.

Next, Thomas had to help Gordon. Thomas chuffed this way and that, looking for the big blue engine, and found him lost on a very rickety branch line.

"The Express line is closed, Gordon! Just keep going!" Thomas peeped. Now he knew where he was, Gordon raced like a rocket to the party.

With all his jobs done, Thomas puffed back to the party, where everyone was having fun, especially The Fat Controller. He was laughing even louder than his brother! And that made Thomas happiest of all.

PERFECT PAIRS

Edward's number is 2. Two things that are the same make a pair. How many pairs can you find on this page?

Answer: there are four pairs — the suitcases, whistles, keys and red flags are in pairs.

HIRO'S JIGSAW ①

Ever since Thomas found him on an abandoned railway, Hiro has enjoyed chuffing around Sodor with his new blue friend. Which piece is missing from this picture of them at the coal hopper?

a

b

c

d

e

f

Answer: piece c is missing.

 Thomas  Charlie  Alicia  The Fat Controller

 had a very special Special. He had to

meet , a singer, at the Docks and take

her to a concert in Maithwaite. But when he

arrived at the Docks, met someone else.

It was  , a new engine from the Mainland.

 gave  his orders. "  , you

must pick up the seats for the concert. If you

need help, ask  ."

After  left,  turned to  .

"Let's race to see who can do their jobs the

fastest," he said.  couldn't let himself

be beaten, so he agreed. When

had climbed aboard Annie and Clarabel,

the race began!

 and  raced across Sodor. Then

there was trouble.  's couplings snapped,

leaving  behind in the carriages. But

 was going so fast he didn't even realise

until he arrived at Maithwaite.

  told him he must go and find

at once as the concert was about to begin.

 puffed away. When he saw ,

he told him what had happened. felt

very bad, so they looked together.

Then,  heard singing!  was

singing for a crowd of people gathered around

her carriage.  was recoupled with

Annie and Clarabel, and he set off for the show

with . When she arrived,

smiled at . "What a fun ride," she said.

"   has made me happy." And with

that,  and beamed at each

other. After all, being Really Useful was much

better than winning a race!

THOMAS' TEASER

These six pictures of Thomas may look the same, but one is different from the others.

Can you find the odd one out?

Answer: picture 4 is the odd one out, as Thomas' number is missing.

TRUE OR FALSE?

How well do you know Thomas and his friends?
Tick ✔ whether the facts below are true or false.

		TRUE	FALSE
1	Rosie has purple paint.	☐	☐
2	Henry can fly.	☐	☐
3	James is a tram.	☐	☐
4	Annie and Clarabel are Edward's carriages.	☐	☐
5	Thomas is number 1.	☐	☐

Answers: 1 – true, 2 – false, 3 – false, 4 – false, 5 – true.

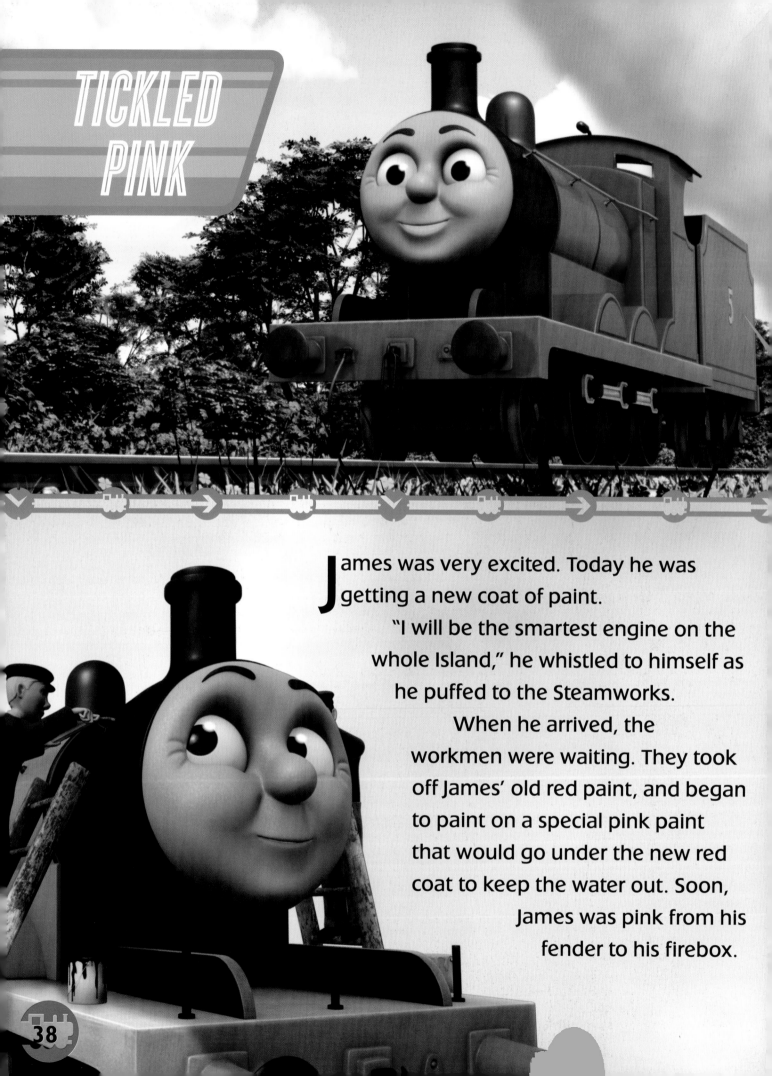

TICKLED PINK

James was very excited. Today he was getting a new coat of paint.

"I will be the smartest engine on the whole Island," he whistled to himself as he puffed to the Steamworks.

When he arrived, the workmen were waiting. They took off James' old red paint, and began to paint on a special pink paint that would go under the new red coat to keep the water out. Soon, James was pink from his fender to his firebox.

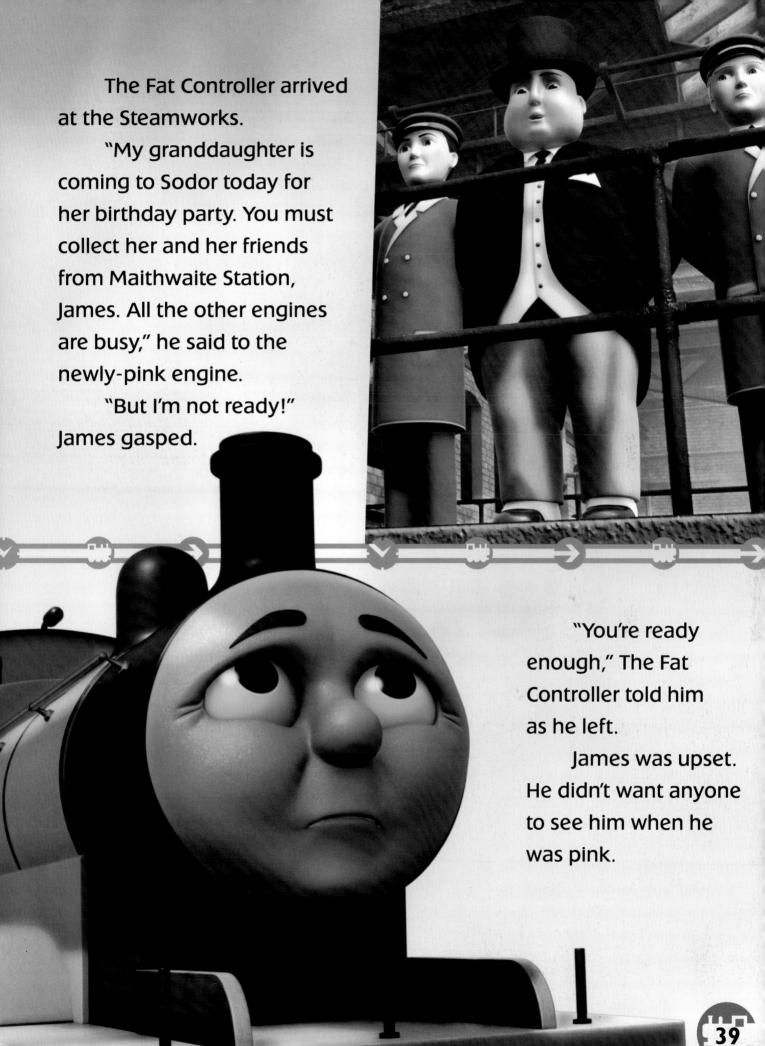

The Fat Controller arrived at the Steamworks.

"My granddaughter is coming to Sodor today for her birthday party. You must collect her and her friends from Maithwaite Station, James. All the other engines are busy," he said to the newly-pink engine.

"But I'm not ready!" James gasped.

"You're ready enough," The Fat Controller told him as he left.

James was upset. He didn't want anyone to see him when he was pink.

He puffed out of the Steamworks feeling very silly indeed. He saw Emily at the junction.

"Cinders and ashes! You're bright pink, James!" she giggled.

James was very embarrassed. He didn't want to be laughed at. Just then, an idea flew into his funnel.

"If I see any other engines, I'll hide!" he said to himself.

So James chugged on across Sodor. He hid behind a willow tree when he saw Toby.

He hid behind some coal trucks when he saw Diesel.

And when he heard Gordon chuffing down the tracks, he backed into a tunnel!

But there was a problem. Gordon wanted to go into the tunnel that James was hiding in! Gordon could see someone was blocking the way, and he was in a rush.

"Express coming through! Come on out!" he huffed angrily.

James stayed still in the tunnel. By now, Thomas and Percy had puffed up too! James knew he had a job to do, and that he would make the other engines and the children late if he didn't hurry! So with a huff and a puff, James chuffed slowly out of the tunnel. All the engines laughed at him.

"I'd hide too if I was bright pink," Gordon tooted.

James hurried off as fast as he could. As he puffed into Maithwaite, he was sure the children would find him funny as well.

But James was in for a surprise. Instead of laughing, The Fat Controller's granddaughter was delighted. Pink was her favourite colour! James couldn't believe how happy it had made her and all her friends.

So the children climbed aboard and they puffed proudly to the Town Hall, just in time for the birthday party.

James the Bright Pink Engine was the hero of the day!

COLOUR JAMES

5 JAMES

Help James get his shiny red paint back. Colour him using your brightest red crayon, then trace over his name below.

James

ODD ONE OUT

Which of these Sodor friends is the odd one out?
Write their name in the box below.

Thomas

Harold

James

Percy

The odd one out is:

Answer: Harold is the odd one out because he is a helicopter. The others are engines.

The children on the Island of Sodor love to smile and wave at Thomas. And he loves to "Peep! Peep!" back!

These pictures may look the same,
but there are 5 differences in picture 2.
Colour a star for each difference you find.

2

BUS

2

Answers: the word 'stop' has disappeared from the sign, the little boy's shorts are now blue, Thomas' face has changed, there is a number 2 on Thomas' side and a kite has appeared in the sky.

THE BIGGEST PRESENT

It was a very special day for all of the engines of Sodor. Hiro was returning to the Island to help with the summer visitors.

That morning, The Fat Controller spoke to Thomas.

"I am going to have a welcome party for Hiro at Knapford," he said. "You must tell all the engines to chuff to Knapford as quickly as possible, Thomas."

But Thomas had other things on his mind. He wanted to get Hiro a special welcome present, too! So he set off to look for a gift and tell everyone about the party.

As he clickety-clacked along the track, an idea flew into Thomas' funnel. He was sure he would find something special at Farmer McColl's Farm! So he pumped his pistons and raced there as quickly as he could.

But when Thomas arrived at the Farm, there was nothing good enough for Hiro's welcome present – just Emily collecting straw. Thomas was so busy looking for a present that he forgot to tell Emily about the party!

Another idea bubbled up from Thomas' boiler.

"The Quarry!" he gasped. "I'm sure I'll find a great present there."

So Thomas huffed happily along until he reached the Quarry.

But when he arrived, there wasn't anything good enough for his old friend Hiro, just Henry shunting slate trucks.

Thomas was so disappointed that he forgot to tell Henry about the party!

Finally, another idea fizzed out of his firebox.

"The Steamworks!" he smiled as he whizzed over the rails. But Thomas was disappointed again; there was only a bell that was too loud. Thomas looked at the clock.

"Bust my buffers," he tooted. "I'd better get going!"

And with that Thomas chuffed away as quickly as his wheels would whirr. He was in such a hurry that he didn't tell Victor or Kevin, who worked at the Steamworks, about the party!

When Thomas raced into Knapford, he saw Hiro waiting alone.

"Cinders and ashes!" Thomas cried. "I didn't tell anyone about the party! And I didn't get Hiro a welcome present! I haven't been Really Useful at all."

Thomas felt terrible, and steamed swiftly out of the Station, leaving behind a very confused Hiro.

Thomas puffed back to Farmer McColl's Farm.

"Emily! Chuff as fast as you can to Knapford. The Fat Controller is having a welcome party for Hiro!" he called before he whooshed to the Quarry.

"You must all steam to Knapford for Hiro's welcome party!" Thomas told Mavis, James, Henry and Toby.

As Thomas whizzed across Sodor, he told everyone he saw about the party. Soon, he rushed back into Knapford, red-faced and all puffed out.

"Thomas, where have you been?" The Fat Controller asked.

"I was trying to find Hiro a special present, but I couldn't find anything. Sorry, Hiro," Thomas tooted, sadly.

Hiro smiled. "But my welcome present is right here! Being with my old friends again is the best present I could wish for," he beamed.

And all of the engines hooted their horns with happiness, because they knew he was right!

CRANES, PLANES AND TRAINS

There are all sorts of Useful machines on the Island of Sodor.

Tick the circle under the pictures to decide whether they are a crane, a plane or a train.

I'm **Thomas**, and my carriages are called Annie and Clarabel.

I'm **Cranky**! I have a long arm but no wheels.

crane   plane   train

crane   plane   train

I'm Gordon, and I pull the Express!

I'm Jeremy! I work at Sodor Airport and I have two wings.

crane   plane   train

crane   plane   train

Answers: Thomas is a train. Cranky is a crane. Gordon is a train. Jeremy is a plane.

TODAY'S DELIVERIES

Thomas and his friends all have special deliveries to make today. Follow the wiggly tracks to find out what they are all delivering.

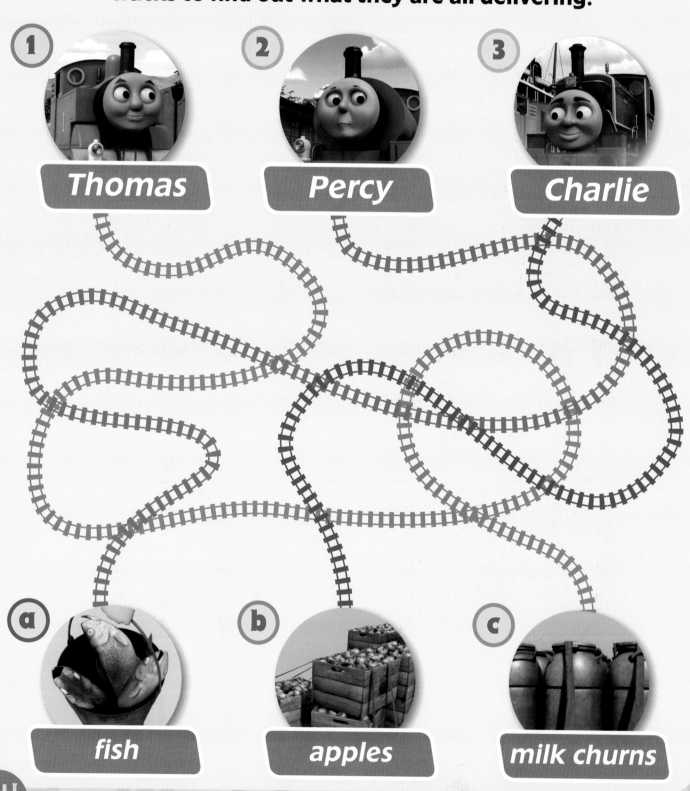

1 **Thomas**

2 **Percy**

3 **Charlie**

a **fish**

b **apples**

c **milk churns**

Answers: Thomas is delivering milk churns, Percy is delivering fish and Charlie is delivering apples.

MISSING LETTER

The same letter is missing from the names of
Thomas' friends, below. Can you work out what it is?
Write it in the blank spaces.

Th_mas

R_sie

Hir_

T_by

Answer: the missing letter is 'o'.

HENRY'S GOOD DEEDS

One day, The Fat Controller came to give the Engines some very important news. A rare bird, called the Sodor Warbler, had arrived back on the Island after a long winter.

"There will be lots of visitors coming to see the bird," The Fat Controller told the engines. "So you must be careful not to frighten it."

"Yes, Sir!" they replied, happily.

"Henry," said The Fat Controller, "you must be Really Useful and deliver a nesting pole for the Warbler to Bluff's Cove."

But Henry was worried about his task – after all, he was such a big engine and the Warbler was just a little bird! But he was determined to be a Really Useful Engine.

Along the way, Henry saw Thomas ahead of him. The little blue engine had stopped to let Farmer McColl's sheep cross the tracks.

"Thank you, Thomas," said Farmer McColl as he followed his sheep. "That was a good deed, well done."

"You're welcome," beamed Thomas.

As Henry watched Thomas chuff cheerfully away, he had an idea.

"I would like to help someone," he said to himself. "Then they will call it a 'good deed' and say 'thank you, Henry!' I'd like that."

So Henry decided that while he was delivering the nesting pole, he would do a good deed as well.

As he puffed along, he saw Farmer Trotter's pigs snuffling by the track. They didn't seem very happy, and kept looking at a muddy field on the other side of the track.

Henry knew just what to do. He put on his brakes, and slowly eased to a stop to let the pigs cross. They looked much happier rolling in the mud!

But Farmer Trotter wasn't happy at all.

"I was taking these pigs to the county show, Henry," he said angrily. "Now they are too muddy."

Henry was very sorry. He hadn't done a good deed after all!

A tooting noise came from the distance. Thomas was rushing towards Henry, carrying visitors to see the Sodor Warbler. But he had to stop for all the pigs.

"Cinders and ashes!" cried Thomas. "The Warbler has been spotted in Fenland Fields. I have to get these visitors there as soon as possible!"

An idea for another good deed flew into Henry's funnel. "I'll take them, Thomas," he said. "It's on my way, and I can get there much faster than you."

Thomas thought this was a very good idea, and so his surprised passengers climbed into Henry's carriages.

Henry whizzed away to Fenland Fields. He arrived in record time, and was very happy to have done a good deed. In fact, he was so happy that he let out a loud whistle of happiness.
TOOT!

Then there was trouble. A beautiful bird flapped and flew from a tree, high into the sky. The visitors let out a groan of disappointment.

"Oh no!" gasped Henry. "That must have been the Sodor Warbler!" He was so upset. He hadn't helped the pigs, Farmer Trotter or the visitors. He hadn't even managed to deliver the nesting pole. Poor Henry was sure no one would ever say "well done" to him now.

A colourful bird fluttered down and rested on Henry's fender as he set off for Bluff's Cove, and Henry smiled at it sadly.

As Henry puffed into the station, he saw the birdwatchers gathered to try and catch a glimpse of the Sodor Warbler. As he got closer, the crowd began to cheer. They smiled, waved, and took photographs of him! It was very strange.

Thomas puffed up next to him.

"Well done, Henry!" Thomas smiled.

"You've brought the Sodor Warbler with you!"

Henry couldn't believe it as he looked down at the little bird. He'd done a good deed after all!

ENGINE FACES

Look at the pictures, then draw lines to match each engine to how they are feeling. One is happy, one is angry, one is sad and one is surprised.

THOMAS

happy

HIRO

angry

VICTOR

sad

HENRY

surprised

Answers: Thomas is surprised. Hiro is happy. Victor is angry and Henry is sad.

Can you match Kevin to the right shadow?

a

b

c

d

LIFT AND LOAD

EXCELLENT EMILY

Sometimes Emily can be a bit of a bossy buffers, but she always gets her jobs done.

Can you find the close-ups below in the big picture? When you find them, tick  **and say "Peep! Peep!" But be careful – one of the close-ups doesn't belong to the picture!**

JOIN THE DOTS

Join the dots to complete this picture of Thomas, before colouring him using your brightest blue. Then wave goodbye!

THOMAS